Bedtime Tales

bookoli

Contents

I Love You More Than...

Marcy Kelman

Gareth Llewhellin

"Just **how much** do you love me?"

Little Tiger sighed.

"I love you more than anything!" Mama replied.

"Do you love me more than a **mouse loves cheese?**"

"Do you love me more than **bears love honey?**"

"Yes! I love you **more than** a chocolate bunny."

"Yes! I love you **more than** a roller-coaster ride."

"Do you love me more than a pirate loves his ship?"

"Do you love me more than **polar bears** love the cold?"

"Yes! I love you **more than** leprechauns love gold."

"Do you love me more than lions like to roar?"

"Yes! I love you **more than** dancing across the floor."

Little Tiger thought for a while, then broke into a happy smile.

"If you love me **more than** shooting down a slide,

More than racing on a

roller-coaster ride ...

" ... if you love me **more than** pirates love their ships,

And **more than** doing pancake flips ...

"... well, wow! That's a lot!" Little Tiger said with a giggle.

Mama gave him a tickle,

which made Tiger wiggle!

"I'll always **cheer the loudest** at everything you do.

And anything you try,

I'll **always** help you through."

" No words can describe all the **joy** that you bring,

That's why **I** love **you**

more than ...

anything!"

I Love My

Mummy

I love my mummy because she **bounces** on my bed,

And shouts out "Good morning!" before kissing my head.

I **love** my mummy

because when she makes things to eat,

She says if I'm good then

I might get a **treat!**

I **love** my mummy because she helps me get dressed,

And always makes sure that I look my best.

I love my mummy

because she's so **funny**.

When we go to the farm,
she **hops**
like a **bunny**!

I **love** my mummy because she helps me to **bake**. We make **muffins** and **cookies** and a **big** chocolate cake.

I love my mummy because on a rainy day,

She always comes up with

fun games we can play.

I love my mummy because she shows things to me.

And teaches me about all the creatures I see.

I love my mummy

because when I get in a muddle,

She's there to give me a **kiss** and a **cuddle**.

I love my mummy because we always laugh.

When we sing and play in our

bubble bath!

I love my mummy because she **reads** to **me** before bed,

And tells me fun stories

made up in her head.

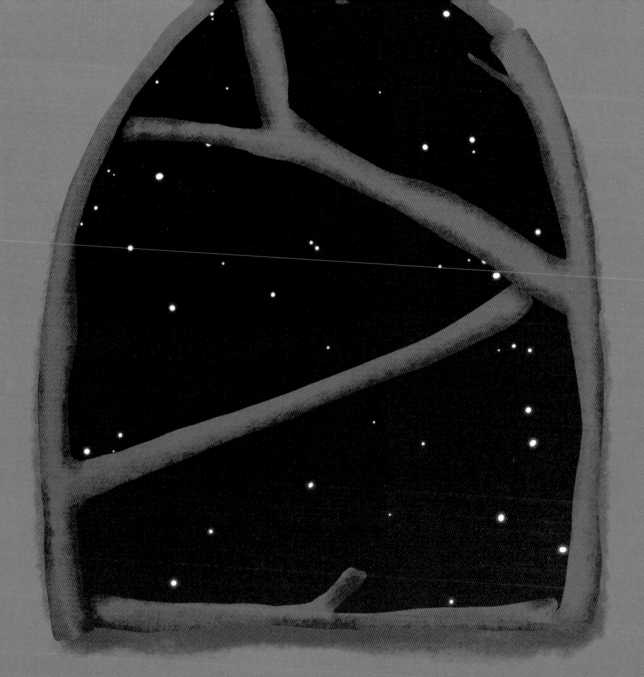

I **love** my mummy because she **hugs** me tight,

Before tucking me in and saying, "**Night**, night."

I love my mummy because

she finds a special way,

To show that she loves me each and every day!

My Daddy and Me

I love my daddy
because in each photograph,

He does something silly
to make us all laugh!

I love my daddy
because he loves to play.
There's no braver knight
with dragons to slay!

I love my daddy
because when I feel blue,

He just seems to know
exactly what to do.

I love my daddy
because he likes to cook.

(Though he never follows
the recipes in the book!)

I love my daddy

because he'll zoom down the slide,

Push us on swings,

and give me a shoulder ride.

I love my daddy
because he can chase a firefly,
Then talk about the moon
and all the planets in the sky.

When we wish upon stars,
that our dreams will come true,
He says, "Who needs wishes?
When I've got you and you and you!"

I love my daddy
because if I scrape my knee,

He's ready with a kiss
and a cuddle for me!

I love my daddy because
when I'm scared at night,

He makes me feels safe
and wraps me up tight.

We talk about shadows
and how they are made.

Thanks to my daddy,
I'm no longer afraid!

I love my daddy
because he loves to nap.

And there's no place cozier,
than snuggled on his lap.

I love my daddy
because I don't need a prize,

To know that he's proud,

I can see it in his eyes.

I love my daddy,
there's nothing he can't do.

And the best thing about him,
is that he loves me too!

Sweet Dreams,

I Love You

"It's getting late,
it's time for bed,
To snuggle up
and rest your head."

Little Otter wants to stay,
he doesn't feel sleepy.
"Can't we play
inside my teepee?"

"Mama is tired.
Mama needs a rest.

"Does your teepee have room for an overnight guest?"

"Yes, of course!
I'll make you a bed,
With a big, comfy quilt
and a pillow for your head."

Mama sees something
hanging overhead,
With feathers and beads
and a web of black thread.

"My dream catcher

grabs the bad dreams

in the night.

Then they all fly away

when it starts to get light.

"And here are the feathers,

which hang over my bed.

They help the good dreams

float into my head."

Little Otter touches the feathers,
a dream starts to swirl.

It's Otter the Astronaut
zooming out of this world!

"Some nights I'm at the circus, flying on a trapeze,

Doing flips in the air, swinging through the breeze.

"Or I'm diving underwater with dolphins and whales,

Getting octopus hugs as I wave to the snails."

"Another dream
is when I'm quite small,

PLAYING CARDS

"And my best friend's a mouse who lives in the wall."

"Another dream I love,"
Otter says, lying back.

"Is floating in a pool
with a drink and a snack."

Then Little Otter gets quiet.

He doesn't make a peep.

As he talks about dreams,

he drifts off to sleep!

"Time to sleep now,
I hope your dreams all come true.

Good night, little one.
Sweet dreams, I love you."